This book belongs to

Bluebell Glade

Dandelion Dell

Heart of Misty Wood

Hawthorn Hedgerows

Heather Hill
Sundown Hill
Golden Meadow
rystal Cave
Moonshine Pond
Dewdrop Spring
Honeydew Meadow
Mulberry Bushes
Misty Wood Rabbit Warren
HOME SWEET HOME

How many **Fairy Animals** books have you collected?

 Chloe the Kitten

 Bella the Bunny

 Paddy the Puppy

 Mia the Mouse

And there are lots more magical adventures coming very soon!

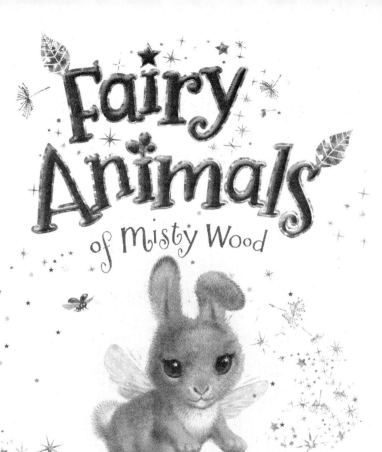

Fairy Animals
of misty Wood

Bella the Bunny

Lily Small

EGMONT

With special thanks to Thea Bennett

EGMONT
We bring stories to life

Bella the Bunny first published in Great Britain 2013
by Egmont UK Limited
The Yellow Building, 1 Nicholas Road, London W11 4AN

Text copyright © 2013 Hothouse Fiction Ltd
Illustrations copyright © 2013 Artful Doodlers Ltd
All rights reserved

ISBN 978 1 4052 6035 0
1 3 5 7 9 10 8 6 4 2

www.egmont.co.uk

www.hothousefiction.com

www.fairyanimals.com

A CIP catalogue record for this title is available from the British Library

Printed and bound in Great Britain by The CPI Group

50045/1

MIX
Paper
FSC   FSC® C018306

Contents

Chapter One: The Talking Bud   1

Chapter Two: A Sad Ladybird   20

Chapter Three: Wanted! Spots!   35

Chapter Four: Daydreaming   51

Chapter Five: Magic Toadstools   63

Chapter Six: Moonshine Pond
                  to Heather Hill   80

Chapter Seven: Loop-the-loop!   103

CHAPTER ONE
The Talking Bud

Spring had come to Misty Wood. As the early morning sun climbed through the bright blue sky, he could see lots of baby plants starting to grow on the ground below.

With a warm smile, the sun reached out his beams to help the plants push through the soil.

High among the trees there was a flash of silver. It was a little bunny! She had soft, silver-grey fur, violet eyes that sparkled like jewels . . . and a pair of golden fairy wings. Her name was Bella and she was a Bud Bunny – one of the fairy animals who lived in Misty Wood. As she flitted through

THE TALKING BUD

3

the trees she sang a song about the special job she was going to do, opening the beautiful spring flowers.

'Shine on, shine on, big bright sun!
I'm on my way to have some fun.
I'll be spending happy hours
Turning buds into flowers . . .'

Suddenly, Bella felt something trickle down her fur. Droplets of rain had started to fall! *Pitter-patter* went the raindrops as they

4

bounced off the leaves. Bella smiled as the water tickled her nose. She liked the rain just as much as the sun – it helped the flowers to grow too!

Bella twitched her velvety nose. The leaves and the earth and the new plants smelled lovely in the rain. Everything was green and fresh.

Misty Wood will be even more beautiful when I've done my job! Bella thought. She twirled her

5

wings and did a happy somersault. *Soon there'll be lovely flowers everywhere!*

Just as quickly as it had begun, the rain stopped and the sun was shining again.

'No time to lose,' Bella told herself. 'I must hurry to Bluebell Glade. There are hundreds of bluebells there, just waiting for me to open them.'

She darted off through the trees,

singing some more of her song:

'Little buds just wait for me,

I'll come soon to help you be

Pretty flowers fresh and bright,

Blue and yellow, pink and white.'

'Hello, Bella!'

Bella spun round at the sound

of her name. Carla the Cobweb

Kitten was flying along behind

her. Her wings sparkled in the

sunlight as she hurried to catch up.

Carla was Bella's best friend.

She had white fur the same colour as the mist that gathered under the trees – and beautiful spots that looked like chocolate drops.

Carla flew up and the two friends touched noses to say hello.

'I can't stop, I must get to Bluebell Glade,' Bella explained. Then she noticed the little basket Carla was carrying, made from tightly woven flower stems. 'Your basket looks heavy today, Carla.'

'It's full to the brim with dewdrops,' Carla replied proudly.

Just like the Bud Bunnies, the Cobweb Kittens had an important job to do in Misty Wood. Every day, they gathered dewdrops and

hung them on cobwebs so the long threads glittered in the sunlight.

Suddenly, Bella's ears quivered. She could hear a buzzing noise.

Bzzzzzzzz . . . Bzzzzzzzzzzz . . .

'What's that?' Bella said, spinning round.

'Look!' Carla cried.

Bella turned to see what Carla had spotted. A cloud of tiny wings glinted in the sunshine. Hundreds of insects were flying towards them.

A small blue beetle bumped into Bella's nose.

'Oops, sorry!' the beetle squeaked, before whizzing on.

Then a swarm of stripy hoverflies buzzed by.

'Hey, where are you going?' called Carla.

'*Zzzzz* . . . Musssst dassshhhh!' the hoverflies replied, following the beetle.

'I've never seen so many

insects,' Bella told Carla. 'I wonder what's going on?'

A big yellow butterfly fluttered up to them.

'Hello, Mr Butterfly,' Bella said. 'Where are you all going?'

'Today is the Misty Wood Insect Sports Day,' he said. 'I'm the Chief Steward!' He twirled his long antennae grandly.

'Wow!' Bella gasped.

'Insect Sports Day! How

could we have forgotten?' said

Carla. 'It happens every year on

Heather Hill.'

'Do come along. Everyone's

welcome,' the friendly butterfly said before whooshing after the hoverflies.

'Oh, I wish we could go,' Carla sighed. 'Watching the insects race must be so much fun!'

'I know!' said Bella. 'Maybe we can, if we're really quick with our cobwebs and flower buds . . .'

'Great idea!' Carla exclaimed. 'I'd better start hanging up these dewdrops then. Bye, Bella, see

you later at Heather Hill.' Carla rubbed noses with her friend, and flew off towards the edge of the wood where the cobwebs were waiting for their dewdrops.

'Bye!' Bella called after her. Then she set off towards Bluebell Glade, humming her happy song.

When Bella reached the glade she swooped down and landed among the bluebells. Each one had lots of tight green buds just

waiting to be opened. Bella's nose tingled with excitement. When she'd finished her work, the glade would be a sea of blue, and the sweet smell of the flowers would drift all through Misty Wood.

She hopped over to a bluebell stem and twitched her nose against the biggest bud. Very slowly, the petals began to unfurl. Bella hopped back and watched, her whiskers quivering in delight.

This was her favourite part of her job. It was like watching a beautiful present unwrap itself. She held her breath and a pretty blue flower, the same shape as a fairy's cap, burst out.

Bella sang happily as she hopped and bounced her way over to another bud.

'A hippity-hop and a hoppity-hip,
Opening flowers makes me skip!'

Soon she had opened dozens

of bluebells. They tinkled like bells in the breeze, and the glade was filled with their sweet scent.

Then there was just one flower left to open. Bella hopped over to it eagerly. One more flower and then she could go to Insect Sports Day! But just as she placed her velvety nose next to the bud, something very strange happened.

'Please don't!' a voice squeaked.

Bella hopped back on her

heels and stared at the plant in
shock. The voice was coming from
the flower! In all the time she'd
been a Bud Bunny, Bella had
never heard a bud speak to her
before. What was going on?

CHAPTER TWO

A Sad Ladybird

Bella pricked up her ears and listened. Everything was quiet. Maybe she'd imagined the voice. 'After all, buds can't talk, can they?' she said to herself.

She hopped up close to the bluebell again. She was about to touch her nose to the bud when . . .

'Didn't you hear what I said?' the bud squeaked. 'Please, please leave me alone!'

Bella jumped back in surprise. She definitely hadn't imagined the voice this time.

'Don't open me,' the flower said. Its voice was quivery now, as if it was about to cry.

21

'Why ever not?' Bella asked.

The bud went quiet again.

Bella leaned up close. 'Don't you want to be a pretty flower?' she whispered.

The bud made a noise that sounded like a sigh. Then it said, in a teeny tiny voice, 'Well . . . the thing is . . .'

'I can't hear you,' Bella said.

The voice spoke again, a bit louder now. 'The thing is, you

see . . . I like being a bud. I don't
want to change.'

Bella's ears shot up and her
eyes opened wide. She couldn't
believe what the flower was saying.
'Don't be silly!' she said. 'You'll be
a beautiful bluebell!'

'No!' squeaked the bud.

But Bella's nose was already
twitching. The bud was probably
just shy. Once she had opened it,
and the flower saw how lovely it

looked, it would soon change its mind. She pressed her nose against the bud and wiggled it.

One by one, the shiny blue petals unpeeled to reveal the biggest, brightest bluebell in the whole glade.

'There, see. You're beautiful!' Bella cried, clapping her silky paws together.

'No!' the voice wailed. 'I'm not beautiful at all. Look at me!'

A SAD LADYBIRD

Something flew out of the flower, zoomed towards Bella and landed on her nose. Bella squinted her eyes to see what was there.

It was a tiny ladybird! With a tiny frown on her face.

'Why didn't you listen to me?' the ladybird whispered. 'Why couldn't you leave me in there?'

'I'm really sorry.' Bella's ears flopped down over her face, the way they always did when she felt upset. 'I . . . I thought it was the flower talking.'

'But flowers don't talk!' the ladybird exclaimed.

'I know, but . . .' Now Bella frowned. 'What were you doing

hiding inside a flower?'

The ladybird looked sad. 'I was hiding from Insect Sports Day.'

'What? But why?' Bella asked. 'The sports day is fun. I'm going to see it with my friend Carla.'

The ladybird flew down from Bella's nose and landed on top of the bluebell in front of her.

'How can I go when I look like this?'

Bella stared at the ladybird.

'What's wrong?' she asked. 'You look all right to me.'

The ladybird sighed. 'How many spots can you see?'

Bella peered closely. The little insect was as red and shiny as a juicy apple. Right in the middle of her back was a single black spot.

'Oh!' Bella said. 'You only have *one* spot.'

The ladybird's eyes filled with tears. 'Exactly! How can I go to

the sports day with just one spot?
I'll look stupid!'

'It's a *nice* spot,' Bella said.

But the ladybird shook her
head. '*Proper* ladybirds have lots of
spots. I'm the only ladybird I know
with just one. My family know
I'm different – they love me all the
same. I don't even mind when my
friends call me One-Spot. But –'
the ladybird had to stop and catch
her breath – 'if I go to the sports

29

day, *all* the insects in Misty Wood will see me and they'll laugh.' The ladybird's lip trembled. Her eyes were bright with tears.

'Don't be sad,' Bella said.

'How can I not be sad?' the ladybird replied.

Bella's violet eyes lit up. 'I know – I'll help you find some more spots!'

The ladybird looked confused. 'How will you do that?'

'Hmm. Let me think.' Bella crouched down and leaned her head to one side to help her brain work better. She wiggled her

nose – sometimes that helped her think too. Suddenly her whiskers twitched and she hopped in the air.

'We need a song! I never do anything without a song.'

Bella hopped and skipped round the little insect. Then she started to sing, thumping her paws on the ground to keep the rhythm.

'This ladybird needs some spots!

Hoppity, hoppity, hop!

We're going to find lots and lots!

32

A SAD LADYBIRD

Hoppity, hoppity, hop!

Hopping here and hopping there,

Hopping, bopping everywhere.

She'll be happy when she's got . . .

LOTS AND LOTS OF SPOTS!'

'How was that?' Bella asked,
giving an extra-bouncy hop as she
finished singing.

But there was no reply.

The ladybird had vanished!

CHAPTER THREE

Wanted! Spots!

'Don't worry, I'm up here!' a little
voice cried from high in the air.

Bella peered into the sky.

The ladybird zoomed down
past her nose. 'Wheeee!' she

squealed, whizzing up again and making a big circle in the air.

'Wow! Loop-the-loops!' Bella cried, sitting up on her hind legs

to watch as the tiny insect whizzed round again.

'I always do loops when I'm happy,' said the ladybird, swooping down to rest on a bluebell stem. 'I'm so excited you're going to help me. Thank you!'

'You're welcome. I'm excited too! By the way, my name is Bella.'

'I'm Lexi!' said the ladybird.

'It's lovely to meet you, Lexi. Right. Let's get started,' Bella said.

'Hurray!' said Lexi, swinging from the bluebell stem, her eyes shining.

'Now, let me think.' Bella tilted her head and wiggled her nose. 'Spots . . . spots . . .' she muttered to herself. 'Where can we find some spots?'

Then she jumped up, her long whiskers quivering. 'I know! My best friend Carla's got lots of beautiful spots. Let's go and ask

her where they came from.'

Lexi didn't say anything. She looked down at the ground.

'What's wrong?' Bella asked.

'I'm scared.' Lexi's voice shook as she spoke. 'We might bump into some of the insects who are going to the sports day. They'll laugh at my one stupid spot, and . . . oh . . . it'll be awful!'

'Don't be afraid!' Bella said kindly. 'We'll think of something.'

39

She leaned her head to one side
again to think. How could they
find Carla without Lexi being seen?
One of Bella's long ears flopped
down and touched the ground.

Bella grinned. She had the
answer! 'Look, Lexi.' Bella lifted
her silky ear with her paw. 'You
can hide under here.'

'Ooh, yes!' Lexi flew over and
crawled under Bella's ear. There
was lots of room, and as Lexi

nestled into Bella's soft fur, she felt cosy and safe.

Bella gently flapped her golden fairy wings and floated up into the sunlight. She headed for the edge of Misty Wood, where the cobwebs hung thickly on the tall hedgerows. That's where Carla would be.

Carla looked very surprised when she saw Bella. 'I thought you were

going to Bluebell Glade,' she said.

'I was – and I did – but I
need to ask you something,' Bella
replied, fluttering down to land
beside her friend. 'Something
really important.'

Carla blinked her big green
eyes. She looked puzzled. 'All right.
Just let me finish this.'

Bella watched as Carla hung
some of her dewdrops on a cobweb
that stretched along the top of

the hedge. The dewdrops shone and sparkled and the spider silk glittered like a diamond necklace.

'What's happening?' Lexi whispered. 'I can't see.' She started wriggling about under Bella's ear.

'Shh!' Bella whispered. 'And keep still. You're tickling me!'

Carla glanced round. 'I'm not tickling you,' she said, looking confused. 'How can I be tickling you when I'm over here hanging

up my dewdrops?'

Bella frowned. 'No, not you. I – I meant my nose was tickling me. I think I need to sneeze.' She rubbed her nose with her front paws.

'Are you OK?' Carla's dark eyes widened with concern.

'I'm fine, look.' Bella hopped and skipped a couple of steps, just to prove it.

Carla placed her basket on the mossy ground. 'So, what did you

want to ask me?'

'Well, we . . . I mean, *I* was wondering, where did you get your spots?' Bella asked.

'My spots?' Carla looked down at the chocolate-coloured markings on her snowy white fur.

'Yes. They're so lovely. Where did they come from?' Bella said.

'I've always had them – ever since I was a tiny kitten,' Carla replied. 'I've no idea where they came from.'

Bella heard Lexi sigh under her ear.

'Don't worry,' whispered Bella

46

to Lexi. 'We'll find someone in Misty Wood who can help.'

'Help with what?' Carla stared at Bella.

'Oh, nothing! Thank you for trying, Carla. See you soon!' Bella hopped away along the hedgerow.

'Bye!' called Carla, still looking confused. 'See you later, at Insect Sports Day!'

Bella patted her ear to check that Lexi was safely tucked away,

then, with a rustle and a shimmer of her golden wings, she took off and soared towards the middle of Misty Wood.

Honeydew Meadow spread out below them. Bella could see some golden Pollen Puppies darting about like sunbeams as they did their special job, spreading the pollen to make the flowers grow. But not one of the puppies had any spots.

Next, Bella flew towards
Dandelion Dell. In the clearing
next to the dell she caught sight
of something moving. It was a
graceful Dream Deer with long

legs and huge eyes. His smooth
brown coat and gauzy wings were
dappled all over with silvery spots.

'I think I've found someone!'
Bella cried. 'Hang on tight, Lexi!'

She fluttered down to where
the deer was nibbling on the sweet
spring grass. Surely, if anyone
could help Lexi, it would be him.

CHAPTER FOUR
Daydreaming

The Dream Deer lifted his nose
from the grass and gazed at Bella
with kind brown eyes.

'Are you searching for a
dream, little bunny?' he asked.

Like all of the fairy animals in Misty Wood, the Dream Deer had their own special job. When the other animals were sleeping the deer brought them happy dreams.

Bella yawned. The deer's voice was so soft and gentle it made her feel like having a nap. She flopped down on to the grass.

'Oh, dear,' she said, 'I think I'm falling asleep!'

'No!' Lexi cried in her ear.

'Please do,' the deer said in his velvety voice. 'I have a lovely dream for you.'

'Noooo!' Lexi cried again.

But as Bella's eyes closed, the ladybird's voice began to fade. The Dream Deer's magic was working.

Bella dreamed she was opening buds, high in the treetops. But she'd never seen flowers like these before. They were huge, white blossoms, hanging like brightly shining moons . . .

53

'Please don't go to sleep!' a little voice squeaked in Bella's ear. 'What about my spots?'

But Bella was lost in her dream and she didn't hear Lexi at all.

. . . now she could see that the white flowers were dotted with gold and yellow and silver. They had lots and lots of beautiful spots . . .

'Spots!' Bella called, opening her eyes and jumping up.

'Hurray!' Lexi cried.

54

The deer looked at Bella, surprised. 'Didn't you like your dream?' he asked.

'I loved it,' Bella told him. 'But I can't sleep now. I need to find some spots. Where did *your* spots come from?'

The deer flicked his tail and turned his long neck to look at the silvery spots on his fur and wings.

'I don't know,' he said. 'They've always been there.'

Bella heard Lexi give another sad little sigh in her ear. She tried not to show the deer how disappointed she was. 'Oh well, thank you, anyway. And thanks for the lovely dream.'

The deer smiled warmly. 'I'm very sorry I wasn't able to help you,' he said. 'I do hope you find some spots, whatever they are for.' Then he leaped gracefully into the air and soared away.

'What are we going to do now?' Lexi whispered.

'I don't know,' Bella said. She was beginning to feel a *tiny* bit worried, too.

'You could try another song,'

57

Lexi suggested.

'Good idea.' Bella jumped up
and began hopping along a little
path that led through the trees.
Lexi snuggled back under her ear.
After a moment, Bella began to sing:

> *'Hop-a-long, hop-a-long,*
>
> > *hoppity-hop!*
>
> *We're looking for someone to*
>
> > *give us some spots!*
>
> *A Dream Deer couldn't help us,*
>
> *And nor could a kitten!*

So we're searching the wood,

For where they are hidden!'

Bella kept on hopping and singing. The path led deep into the Heart of Misty Wood. The trees grew close together and the ferns and moss were thick and green. Bella felt a little afraid. Apart from her song, this part of the wood was silent. There was no one around, and no sign of *any* spots!

Oh, dear. I must be going the

wrong way, Bella thought.

She was about to turn and hop back when a ray of sunshine lit the path ahead. The trees were thinning to form a clearing.

Bella came to a halt, her heart beating fast. There was a

ring of bright red toadstools in the clearing.

'Why have you stopped?' Lexi asked.

Bella lifted up her ear so that Lexi could see the toadstools.

'Mushrooms?' Lexi said. 'How

can mushrooms help us?'

'They're not mushrooms . . .
they're *toadstools*!' Bella explained.

Lexi still looked very puzzled.

'It's a magic toadstool ring!'
Bella whispered. 'A place where
wishes come true!'

And, without another word,
she hopped out of the trees and flew
straight to the middle of the ring.

CHAPTER FIVE

Magic Toadstools

It was very quiet in the middle of the toadstool ring. There were no birds singing at all, and even the leaves in the trees had stopped rustling. Bella gave a little shiver,

but she knew she must be brave.
She lifted her ear right up.

'Come and sit beside me,' she
whispered to Lexi.

'Why?' Lexi asked.

'We need to close our eyes,'
Bella explained. 'Then I'll make a
wish for you to have some spots.'

'Oh, I hope it works,' breathed
Lexi.

Bella closed her eyes tight and
thought for a moment. As soon as

the words came into her head, she began to sing:

'*Lexi's only got one spot,*

Which makes her feel so sad –

But grant my wish, kind toadstools

And she'll be very glad!'

Bella stopped singing and listened. There was still no sound. Not even the faintest breeze or quietest birdsong. But then . . . *swoosh!*

Something ruffled against her.

'What's that?' Lexi squeaked.

Swish! Swoosh!

There it was again! It felt
like a big, soft brush was stroking
Bella's fur.

'Don't move!' Bella whispered
to Lexi. 'It's the magic. You have to
keep your eyes closed.'

Suddenly, the swooshing
stopped. Everything was quiet.

Bella opened one eye and saw

the ring of toadstools. Then she

opened her other eye.

'Oh, no!' she gasped when she

saw Lexi.

'Oh, no!' squeaked Lexi when

she saw Bella.

'What's wrong?' they both

said at exactly the same time.

'You've got spots!' Bella said.

'But . . .'

'So have you,' interrupted

Lexi. 'Big white ones!'

Bella stared at the ladybird. 'Yours are white too!'

'They can't be!' Lexi cried.

'It's true,' Bella said. 'Let's go and look in that puddle over there.'

They fluttered over to look at their reflections in the water.

'It *is* true!' Lexi said. 'I've got lots and lots of *white* spots. But they should be black.'

Bella gazed at her friend. The ladybird did look strange, with

one big black spot and lots of little

white ones. Then Bella leaned

over to look at her own reflection.

'Oh, my!' she exclaimed.

There were big white blobs all over her silky grey fur. She didn't look like her usual self at all.

Lexi started to cry. Tiny trails of tears glimmered as they trickled down her face. 'I c-can't go to the sports day like this! What are we going to do?'

'Don't worry,' Bella said. 'This toadstool ring is definitely magic, but I must have sung the wish

wrong. Let me try again.'

Bella started flying back towards the ring but Lexi stayed where she was.

'Why aren't you coming?' Bella asked.

'The magic might go wrong again,' Lexi replied. 'I might end up with purple spots. Or spots every colour of the rainbow. And that would be even worse!'

'I'm sure that won't happen,'

Bella said, flying back over to Lexi. 'I just have to get the wish right, that's all.'

Lexi gave a little nod and she fluttered back to the toadstool ring.

When they were both in the ring again they closed their eyes. Bella tilted her head, wiggled her nose, and then she started singing:

'I should have asked for black spots!

Can the white ones disappear?

Lexi needs some black ones,

Oh, I do hope you can hear!'

Misty Wood was silent again. Had the song worked? Bella opened one eye to take a peek. Lexi's spots were still white! The toadstools had worked their magic the first time, why weren't they listening now? Bella took a deep breath and bellowed at the top of her voice:

'Listen, toadstools in your ring,

Can't you hear me when I sing?

Lexi needs some BLACK SPOTS

And –'

'There's no need to shout,' a deep voice interrupted.

Bella's fur stood on end and Lexi squeaked with fright. They both kept their eyes shut tight. Maybe the magic was working?

'I don't do black spots,' the voice said. 'I only do white.'

That doesn't sound very magical, Bella thought. She opened her eyes.

A large red fox was sitting in front of them. He was holding a lily pad full of white paint.

'Are you *sure* you only do white spots?' Lexi said.

'Quite sure,' said the fox, nodding his head.

'Sorry,' said Bella. 'But Lexi needs *black* spots.'

'Yes,' said Lexi. 'I'm a ladybird, you see.'

The fox stood up and shook himself. 'Watch this,' he said. Then he trotted over to the edge of the ring with his lily pad. He dipped

his tail in the paint and dabbed one of the red toadstools until it was covered with white spots.

'See?' he said. 'That's my job. Putting the white spots on the toadstools.'

'Gosh – that looks lovely,' Bella said. 'Much better than plain red toadstools.'

'Thanks,' the fox said with a smile. 'I'm really sorry I'm not able to help you. And don't worry,

the spots will wash off. I have to re-paint these toadstools every time it rains.'

He picked up his lily pad and moved on to the next toadstool.

'Goodbye, Mr Fox,' Bella said. 'Thank you for trying to help us. Come on, Lexi.'

'Where are we going?' Lexi asked as she settled down in Bella's soft fur.

'Moonshine Pond,' Bella told

her. 'We'll wash away these white spots and then we'll think of what to do next.'

'OK!' squeaked Lexi as the bunny opened her golden wings and fluttered into the air. 'Let's go!'

CHAPTER SIX

Moonshine Pond to Heather Hill

'The pond looks so bright and beautiful today,' Bella cried, as she spotted the gleaming water through the trees. 'The Moonbeam

Moles have been busy.'

Every night the moles caught moonbeams and dropped them into Moonshine Pond to make it glow like the moon itself.

Bella landed on the grassy bank. 'OK, Lexi, time to wash off those spots,' she called, lifting up her ear so Lexi could fly out.

Lexi landed on the bank and looked down at the silvery water.

'What if they don't wash off,'

she said nervously.

'Oh, I'm sure they will. Look.'
Bella dipped a paw in the edge
of the pond. The fox was right –
the water washed the white blobs
clean away.

'Yippee!' Lexi cried, and she
did a quick loop-the-loop before
diving head first into the water.

Bella hopped in too and
splashed and splashed until all the
spots were gone.

'That's better!' she cried,

leaping on to the bank and

shaking out her fur and wings.

'You look like a proper Bud Bunny again!' said Lexi, crawling out from the water. 'Have my spots gone, too?'

'They have,' Bella replied. 'Only the black one's left.'

'I'd better dry myself off,' Lexi said. She flew up into the air, whirring her little wings as she looped-the-loop.

Bella sat down on the grass. She felt really sad that she hadn't

been able to help Lexi, but it was lovely to rest in the sunshine. She could feel the warm rays drying her fur.

'Wheeee!' came Lexi's voice from high up in the air.

Bella looked up and smiled. Lexi must be feeling very happy that the white spots were gone. She was looping-the-loop again and again.

Then Bella saw a large yellow

85

butterfly fluttering through the trees. It was the same one that she and Carla had met that morning.

'Hello again!' the butterfly said, landing on the grass.

'Hello, Mr Butterfly. I thought you were going to the sports day,' Bella said.

'It's just about to start,' the butterfly explained. 'As Chief Steward, it's my job to make sure no insects get left behind.

I wouldn't want anyone to miss it!'

Then he saw Lexi looping-the-loop.

'My, oh my, little ladybird, what wonderful flying!' he called. 'With talent like that you should be racing in the sports day. Quick, come with me.'

Bella was about to explain that Lexi was too shy, but it was too late. The butterfly had leaped into the air.

'Oh, no, no, no!' squealed Lexi, zooming up to the top of her loop as the butterfly approached.

But the butterfly was in such a hurry that he didn't hear her. He scooped Lexi up in his long legs and swooped off through the trees.

Bella twitched her nose in confusion. Everything had happened so quickly. One moment Lexi was happily looping-the-loop and the next moment she was gone!

Bella whirled her shining golden wings and flew after the butterfly as fast as she could.

'Don't worry, Lexi!' she shouted, as she took off. 'I'm coming!'

'Wow!' Bella gasped as she saw Heather Hill.

Everything was ready for Insect Sports Day. There was a circular flying track for the beetles

and the ladybirds, with lots of
obstacles for them to get over.
Flowers had been laid out to make
a nectar-gathering marathon for
the bees. There was a high jump
for the grasshoppers, a cobweb
trapeze for the spiders, and some
fireflies were marking out an area
in the sky for the butterflies' races.

All around the edge of the
arena, fairy animals were taking
their places, excitedly waiting for

the sports day to begin. The Pollen Puppies were wagging their tails so fast they blurred. The Stardust Squirrels were scampering about, sprinkling stardust until the heather glittered silver in the sun.

Bella saw a group of Cobweb Kittens sitting under a large oak tree. She wondered if her friend Carla was here already, but she couldn't stop and check now. She had to find out if Lexi was OK.

Bella dived down into
the crowd of insects that were
hurrying about, and pushed her
way to the front.

She spotted the yellow butterfly
at the start of the flying track.
Lexi was with him. She looked
scared. Bella wished there was
something she could do to help her.

Three other young ladybirds
were there, too. They were wearing
leg bands with numbers on them

– one, two and three. Ladybird
Three was holding a fourth band
and looking worried.

'What shall we do?' he said to the butterfly. 'The fourth member of our team has hurt his wing and won't be able to race.'

'Aha!' the butterfly said. 'No need to worry. It just so happens that I have found a ladybird so fast, so fantastic, and so fabulous at flying she will make the perfect fourth member of your team.' The butterfly twirled his antennae with a flourish. 'This is Lexi. Your new

Number Four!'

'Yay!' The three ladybirds whooped and buzzed.

Bella held her breath. She wondered if they would notice that Lexi only had one spot. Lexi was obviously wondering the same thing. She was hopping from one tiny foot to the other. But the other ladybirds didn't seem to notice at all.

'You're the most important member of the team,' the butterfly

told Lexi. 'Number Four does the last lap of the race. If you win, you'll be the star of the sports day.'

He fixed the number four band on to Lexi's leg. Lexi fluttered her wings nervously.

'The Obstacle Relay Race is on!' the butterfly cried. 'Ladybirds against beetles. Good luck!'

'Be brave, Lexi,' Bella called. 'You'll be great!' She hoped Lexi could hear her.

Just at that moment, a baby caterpillar, who was sitting on his Moth Mummy's back, noticed Lexi waiting behind the start line.

'Look!' he said in a loud, surprised voice. 'That ladybird's only got one spot!'

Bella groaned. Poor Lexi! She was quite close to the little caterpillar so she must have heard what he said. But there was nothing Bella could do.

The yellow butterfly was giving his instructions to the ladybird team. He held up a grass seed. 'Here's your baton. Pass it to the next ladybird as you finish your lap. If you don't, the team will be disqualified.'

Ladybird One took the grass seed in his antennae and fluttered up to the start. He lined up next to a small green beetle.

'Ready?' the butterfly asked.

The ladybird and the beetle nodded.

'Steady!' called the butterfly.

A bumblebee flew forward.

'*ZZZZ*! GO!' she buzzed.

The two little insects flew off so fast that their wings began to hum. They headed for the first obstacle – a huge pile of sticks.

Bella looked back at Lexi and saw that her friend was sitting on the ground looking very frightened

indeed. With a quick hop and a skip, Bella made her way to the front until she was standing right next to Lexi.

'Wow, this is so exciting!' Bella said. 'Three laps and then it'll be your turn!'

Quivering with fear, Lexi held her front legs over her eyes. 'I can't do it, Bella,' she said. 'Everyone will laugh at me. What am I going to do?'

CHAPTER SEVEN

Loop-the-loop!

The yellow butterfly hovered in
the air. He was holding a bright
orange mushroom shaped like a
trumpet. 'They're off!' he shouted
into the mushroom. His voice

echoed all over Heather Hill. 'The ladybird and the beetle are coming up to the first obstacle – The Sticks! And they're over!'

Bella looked down at Lexi.

Lexi was still covering her eyes.

The rest of the crowd were very excited. All the ladybirds jumped up and down. 'That's our boy!' they yelled.

The beetles jumped up and down, too. 'Faster!' they shouted to

the green beetle. 'Go go go!'

Behind her, Bella could hear
the Pollen Puppies yelping with
joy. She looked back at the race.

The beetle was just entering the Cobweb Tunnel.

'Touch those sides and you'll stick fast!' the butterfly cried.

Bella's whiskers twitched with excitement as the ladybird reached the tunnel.

'Number One's just about to go in,' she said to Lexi, 'but he's behind the beetle.'

'The beetle's way out in front! He's at the last obstacle!' shouted

106

the butterfly. 'There he goes – up the Helter-Skelter Tree!'

'This bit looks really exciting,' Bella said to Lexi as Beetle One flew round and round between the branches of a tall tree. But Lexi still wouldn't uncover her eyes.

Bella's heart pounded as the beetle bumped into some branches. But he made it to the bottom safely and back to the start line.

'Now Beetle Two's got the

107

baton and he's racing into the lead!' the butterfly shouted.

Ladybird One was a long way behind as he flew up to the start, holding out the grass seed for Ladybird Two.

The second ladybird was faster than the first. She raced through the tunnel so quickly, she came out ahead of the beetle!

Bella thumped her paws in glee. Ladybird Two was brilliant!

'Look, Lexi!' she begged.

'She's overtaken the beetle!'

But Lexi still wouldn't look.

The butterfly roared into his

mushroom trumpet: 'Ladybird

Two is coming up to the finish –

now Ladybird Three is off!'

Bella turned to Lexi. 'It's you next! Come on!'

'No, I can't!' squeaked Lexi.

Bella's ears drooped in despair. How, oh, how could she get Lexi to race? Then she had an idea. Bella snuggled up close to her friend, and she started singing a new song, very softly, so that only Lexi could hear.

'It doesn't matter a jot

110

That you've only got one spot.

You can do it if you try,

All you have to do is fly!'

Lexi opened her eyes and stared at Bella. 'Do you really think I can do it?'

Bella smiled and nodded. 'Of course you can. You're wonderful at flying.'

Lexi gave a big sigh. Then, very slowly, she stepped out on to the start line. Everyone could see

her one black spot now.

Bella knew how afraid Lexi
was that everyone would laugh.
But the crowd weren't looking
at Lexi. They were all pushing
forward to see Ladybird Three as
she finished her lap. She was out in
front!

'Come on, ladybirds!' yelled
the butterfly. 'Number Three's in
the lead! All she has to do is hand
over to Ladybird Four . . . Oh, no!'

There were so many creatures milling around at the starting line that Ladybird Three couldn't see who to pass the baton to. She circled in the air, searching for the fourth member of the team.

'This way!' Bella shouted. 'Look for One-Spot Lexi!'

The sun shone down on Lexi and her single black spot. *Now* Ladybird Three knew who to head for! She whizzed down towards

Lexi, holding out the grass-seed baton.

'Go, Lexi, go!' shouted Bella with a big grin.

Lexi seized the baton in her antennae and zoomed away. She was over The Sticks in a flash – with a spectacular loop-the-loop. The crowd went wild, cheering and clapping, and the Pollen Puppies wagged their tails faster than ever.

'We're on the last lap now –

the beetles are in the lead again – but just look at that!' howled the butterfly. 'The ladybird's at the tunnel already!'

Lexi shot through the Cobweb Tunnel like an arrow. She was catching up to Beetle Four!

'This is amazing!' the butterfly gabbled. 'Just look at One-Spot Lexi! She's looping-the-loop all the way up the Helter Skelter!'

'Go, Lexi, GO!' yelled Bella.

'I've never seen anything like it!' the butterfly shrieked. 'She's fantabulous! She's brilltastic! She's right behind the beetle . . .'

Bella hopped up and down, clapping her front paws together as Lexi hurtled towards the finish. Now she was in front of the beetle!

'Go, One-Spot Lexi! Go, go, GO!' roared the crowd.

Lexi shot across the finish line.

'Yes!' cried the butterfly, throwing his trumpet in the air and catching it. 'She's done the fastest time ever! A Misty Wood record. The ladybirds have won!'

'I did it!' Lexi panted, circling down to land on the grass in front of Bella.

'You won! You won!' Bella was so proud of her new friend. 'You're a star, Lexi!'

The rest of the ladybird team came up to congratulate Lexi. 'You were incredible!' Ladybird One said. 'We'd never have won without you.'

The yellow butterfly called the

team over to collect their prizes.
He gave each ladybird an acorn-
cup full of golden honey.

'Well done, One-Spot Lexi,' he
said.

Lexi blushed even redder. She
took her honey and hurried back
to Bella.

'Let's get away before they
start laughing at my spot,' she
said, looking around at the
spectators who were still buzzing

119

with excitement over the race.

The two friends fluttered their wings and drifted away over the heather, looking for somewhere quiet. But everywhere they went, insects and fairy animals flew up to congratulate Lexi.

'Hello!' called a Moss Mouse. 'I loved your loop-the-loops!' He tried a clumsy loop of his own before flying off.

'Mmmarvellous!' droned

a furry bee. 'Bbbbessst race evvvvverr!' Then she buzzed away, searching for a flower.

'They're not laughing at me!' Lexi said, looking very surprised.

'Why would they laugh?' Bella said with a smile. She saw a patch of grass in between the heather plants. 'Let's go and sit there so you can eat some of your prize honey.'

'You have to have some too,'

Lexi said. 'If it wasn't for you I'd never have been brave enough to race.'

They flew down, and were just dipping into the acorn when a very small ladybird peeped at them through the heather stalks.

He looked at Lexi shyly. 'Hello, Lexi. You're my hero,' he mumbled, then darted away.

Lexi stared after him. Then she looked at Bella, puzzled. 'Why

would he say that I'm his hero?'

'Because you won the race
for the ladybird team,' Bella said.
'And it wasn't *just* because you're
so good at flying . . .'

'What do you mean?' Lexi asked.

Bella licked a drop of delicious
honey from her paw. 'Well, if you
weren't One-Spot Lexi, Ladybird
Three would never have known
who to pass the baton to.'

Lexi looked thoughtful, then

123

her eyes began to shine. 'You mean . . . it was a *good* thing that I only have one spot?'

Bella nodded. A smile spread slowly across Lexi's face and she whizzed up into the air in a happy loop-the-loop. 'Maybe being different isn't so bad after all,' she called down to Bella. 'Wheeeeeee!'

There was a shimmer of silver wings above the heather, and Carla the Cobweb Kitten fluttered

down to join them.

'Hello, Bella! I've been looking for you everywhere,' she said. 'Did you see the Obstacle Relay Race? It was amazing!'

'Yes,' Bella said proudly. She nodded at Lexi. 'My new friend here just won it.'

'Oh, wow!' Carla looked at Lexi with admiration. 'You were brilliant. I wish I could do loop-the-loops like you.'

'I can teach you if you like,' Lexi said shyly.

'Ooh, really?' Carla fluttered her silver wings excitedly. 'I would love that!'

Carla turned back to Bella. 'Are you still trying to find out where spots come from?'

Bella looked at Lexi.

Lexi smiled and shook her head. She was happy just the way she was.

'Not any more,' Bella said, winking at Lexi. 'No need for any more spots here!'

The sun was starting to hide his face behind the trees of Misty

127

Wood and the sky was turning pinky gold. The warm spring day was coming to an end. It was nearly time to go home.

'Thank you, Bella,' said Lexi. 'Your songs have really helped me today.'

'You're welcome,' Bella said. 'In fact . . .'

Bella began hopping around Lexi and Carla as she started singing another song:

'Making friends with you

Has been the best thing by far.

One-Spot Lexi,

The loop-the-loop star!'

Misty Wood Word Search

Can you find all these words from
the story in this fun word search?

BUNNY
FLOWER
BELLA
PETAL
HOP
SKIP
WINGS
RACE
LEXI

J	Q	C	Q	W	J	P	X	T	C	M	Z	M	N	F
S	W	O	P	F	G	Q	B	C	L	F	P	X	M	Y
T	U	X	T	O	N	F	B	U	N	N	Y	L	V	T
S	Y	C	B	R	W	I	H	V	D	R	Y	C	F	I
W	S	W	V	N	G	K	G	Z	K	X	B	L	Y	E
G	K	R	P	E	R	B	R	A	C	E	E	A	L	C
Z	N	N	I	Z	C	R	I	Z	C	X	R	G	H	C
E	D	C	N	M	N	W	B	Y	K	U	C	W	R	U
L	N	C	J	R	B	H	V	F	A	W	T	X	H	K
S	U	H	N	V	S	D	G	L	H	L	I	H	O	P
H	S	W	A	D	G	F	L	O	W	E	R	N	I	M
U	E	D	Z	E	C	E	E	R	L	I	T	K	G	Q
S	V	Y	D	X	B	M	X	W	G	K	S	L	F	S
O	P	B	N	U	V	E	I	E	W	P	H	A	N	K
U	M	P	E	T	A	L	E	K	L	U	L	L	P	

Help Bella finish her song!

Bella loves singing about Misty Wood! She was making up a new song when she had to hop off to the glade to open some bluebells.
Can you finish Bella's song in the space below?

I love skipping over the hill,
To skip, skip, skip
Gives me a thrill!

I love hopping in the sun,
To hop, hop, hop
Is so much fun!

....

....

....

Help Lexi find her way to the finish line.
Watch out for dead ends!

Fairy Animals
of Misty Wood

Meet all the fairy animal friends!

Chloe the Kitten

Bella the Bunny

Paddy the Puppy

Mia the Mouse

Look out for Hailey the Hedgehog and lots more coming soon . . .

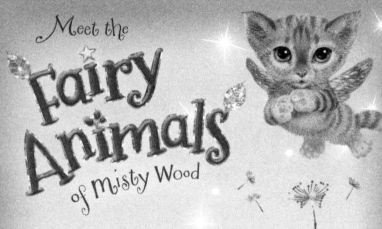